Patches' Easter Adventure

by Hans Wilhelm

BARRON'S

All inquiries should be addressed to:
Barron's Educational Series, Inc.
250 Wireless Boulevard
Hauppauge, New York 11788
www.barronseduc.com

Library of Congress Control Number: 2007923767

ISBN-13: 978-0-7641-6060-8
ISBN-10: 0-7641-6060-5

Printed in China
9 8 7 6 5 4 3 2 1

Philip had a new pet named Puppy,
and a toy bunny he called Patches.
Philip loved his puppy, but he loved Patches even more.
"You're my very, very best friend," Philip often told Patches.
You're my best friend, too, Patches thought.

Philip could not go to the doctor without Patches.
He could not take a bath or brush his teeth
without his little friend at his side.

"Patches needs a good-night kiss, too,"
Philip reminded his mommy every night.

When the light was switched off,
Philip and Patches snuggled up close.

Philip would tell Patches stories and share his secrets.
Patches would listen with all his heart.

Then they would meet in their dreams to have adventures together.

But one day in the spring
everything changed.

That morning Philip and Patches
took Puppy for a walk in the field.
In a little while, it began to rain.

Soon the rain was coming down hard!
Philip grabbed Puppy and ran off
toward home as fast as he could.

That's when Patches fell out of his pocket.
Help! cried Patches as he landed in a puddle.
But Philip was already gone.

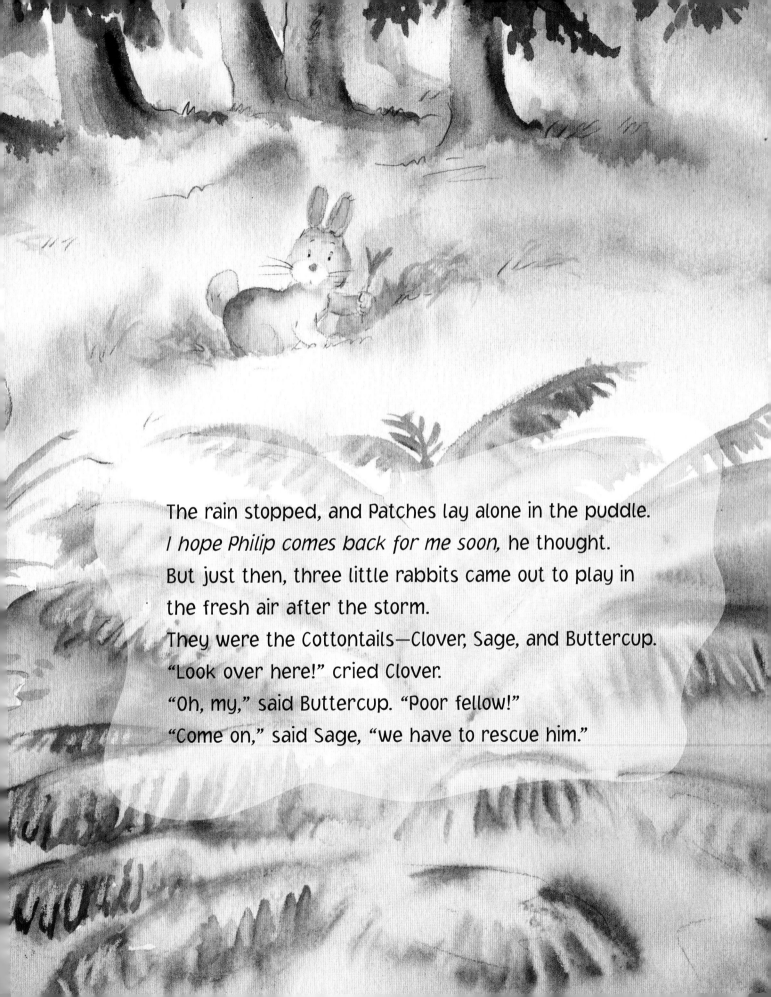

The rain stopped, and Patches lay alone in the puddle.
I hope Philip comes back for me soon, he thought.
But just then, three little rabbits came out to play in
the fresh air after the storm.
They were the Cottontails—Clover, Sage, and Buttercup.
"Look over here!" cried Clover.
"Oh, my," said Buttercup. "Poor fellow!"
"Come on," said Sage, "we have to rescue him."

At their home, the three little rabbits
took good care of Patches.

"You'll soon be up to snuff again," Buttercup said
as they dried him off with a towel.

Sage washed Patches' pants and hung them up to dry.
Then they read him some of their favorite stories.

Patches felt a little better.
But he never stopped
thinking about Philip.

That night Philip looked everywhere for Patches.
"You may have lost him when you took Puppy out,"
said his mom. "We'll look for him in the morning."
It was very difficult for Philip to go to sleep that night.

In the morning, Philip searched the field.
Where could Patches be?
"We'll ask around," Philip's parents said.
"Maybe one of our neighbors found him."
But what if Patches was lost for good?
Philip had never felt so sad and lonely.

"That little fellow looks a bit glum to me," Mr. Cottontail said at breakfast. "He's probably missing someone very much. I think you should take him back where you found him."

"No way!" said Clover. "He's ours.
If someone cared about him, they
would not have left him out in the rain."

That's not true! Patches tried to say.
Philip cares about me.
Please, take me back to Philip!
But the rabbits could not hear the silent
cries of a toy bunny.

So, Patches stayed with the Cottontails.

It wasn't all bad. Clover, Sage, and
Buttercup included him in most of
their games.

Some games were more fun than others.

Patches took it all without complaining.

But not a day went by that he didn't miss Philip.

He knew that Philip was missing him just as much.

One day Mrs. Cottontail said, "Be careful with that bunny! He really doesn't belong to you, you know. I think it's time you took him back where you found him."

Yes, yes! Patches thought.

But the little Cottontails didn't want to give him up.

Then the days got warmer.
Clover, Buttercup, and Sage
couldn't wait to run outside
and play in the sun.

"Come and catch me!"
Buttercup called to Clover
as they ran through
the garden.

What about me? Patches thought.
Aren't you going to take me with you?

Patches watched from the windowsill as the
Cottontails jumped, ran, and turned cartwheels.
Maybe they don't want me any more, Patches thought.

Day after day Patches sat alone on the windowsill.
Philip would never forget me like this.
Patches knew. *How I wish there was a way
I could go back home.*

Then one day, Patches saw the Cottontails carrying paints and brushes and a basketful of eggs to the garden. The whole family—even Clover, Buttercup, and Sage—began to paint the eggs.

It must be Easter time, Patches thought, and he remembered how, every Easter, Philip would get a delivery of brightly colored Easter eggs.

A faint feeling of hope began to stir in Patches' heart.

That night, the Cottontails left the basket of colored eggs inside under Patches' window.

It was just what Patches had been hoping for!

His whiskers stood out straight and began to wiggle.
All his thoughts turned to home—and Philip.
Wishing as hard as he could, the little bunny summoned up all the love in his heart.
That—plus a timely puff of wind—was enough to propel him off the windowsill.

Patches tumbled through the air and landed with a soft thump in the basket with the painted eggs!
So far, so good, he thought.

In the morning, Mr. Cottontail lifted the heavy
basket and strapped it to his back.

"Have a good trip!" said Mrs. Cottontail.
Clover, Sage, and Buttercup waved.
"Happy Easter!" they called.

Luckily, nobody noticed Patches.

But at his first stop, Mr. Cottontail discovered the stowaway.
"Hello, little fellow," he said.
"How did you get here?
I wish I knew where you belonged.
Today would be a great day to take you home."

Take me to the yellow house with the green fence! Patches tried to tell him.
But again, he could not be heard.
So, Mr. Cottontail put him back in the basket and continued his deliveries.

There were hardly any eggs left in the basket when Patches suddenly saw a familiar sight: the yellow house with the green fence! Philip's house! The place where he belonged!

It was also Mr. Cottontail's last stop. Carefully he put the
remaining eggs down on the soft grass. *Put me down, too!*
Patches cried. *Please, this is my home!* But Mr. Cottontail
could not hear him. And with Patches still inside the basket
he hopped off. Then there came a frightful noise!

"Arf! Arf! Arf! Arf!"
It was Puppy! The frightened Easter bunny
jumped over the garden fence to get away.

Thank you! cried Patches as he sailed through the air.
Watch out! Here I come!

And as Patches fell to the ground, he saw
someone come running out of the house.

How happy Philip was when he saw Patches!
And how happy Patches was when
Philip hugged him close.
"The Easter Bunny brought
you back to me!" Philip cried.
"Where have you been?"

Patches wished he could tell Philip
how much he had missed him
and how glad he was
to be back home.
But he knew he
didn't have to.

All that mattered was that they
were together again.